LA ISLA FANTÁSTICA

FANTASTIC ISLAND

Illustrated by Brenda Haw

Adapted from Puzzle Island, in the Usborne Young Puzzles series, by
Kathy Gemmell & Nicole Irving

Bilingual editor: Kate Needam
Design adaptation by John Russell

Language consultants:
Esther Lecumberri & Marta Nuñez

Original story by Susannah Leigh

Edited by Gaby Waters
Designed by Kim Blundell

Contents

About this book

This book is about an apprentice pirate called Max, his pet parrot, Morgan, and their adventures on Fantastic Island. The story is in Spanish and English. You can look up the word list on page 23 if you want to check what any Spanish word means. This list also shows you how to say each Spanish word.

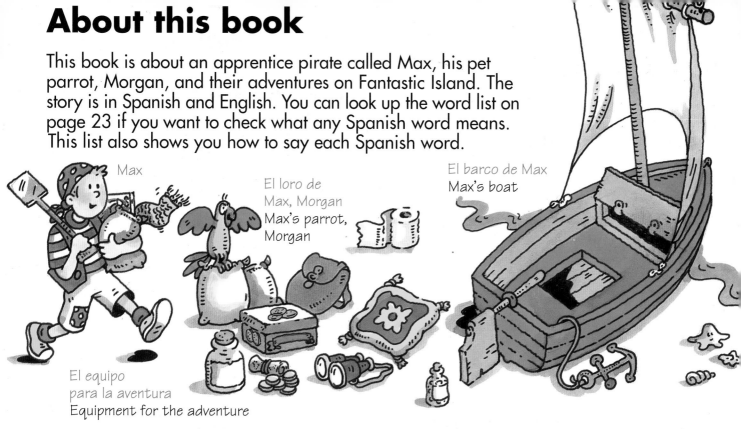

Max

El loro de Max, Morgan
Max's parrot, Morgan

El barco de Max
Max's boat

El equipo para la aventura
Equipment for the adventure

La historia   The story

La insignia con la calavera
Skull and crossbones badge

Para convertirse en un verdadero pirata, Max debe encontrar una insignia con una calavera.
To become a real pirate, Max must find a skull and crossbones badge.

La insignia está escondida en el cofre del tesoro en algún lugar en el corazón de la Isla Fantástica.
The badge is hidden in the treasure chest somewhere at the heart of Fantastic Island.

El cofre del tesoro
Treasure chest

There is a puzzle on every double page. Solve each one and help Max and Morgan on their way. All the Spanish words you need to solve the puzzles are in the word keys (look out for this sign: 🔑). If you get stuck, the answers are on page 22.

Things to look for

During his journey to the treasure chest, Max must collect the nine pieces of pirate kit shown here. One piece of the kit is hidden on every double page. Can you spot them all?

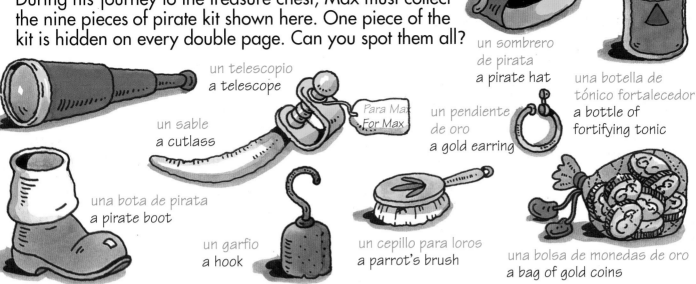

un telescopio
a telescope

un sombrero
de pirata
a pirate hat

una botella de
tónico fortalecedor
a bottle of
fortifying tonic

un sable
a cutlass

*Para Max
For Max*

un pendiente
de oro
a gold earring

una bota de pirata
a pirate boot

un garfio
a hook

un cepillo para loros
a parrot's brush

una bolsa de monedas de oro
a bag of gold coins

Horacio the Horrible

Horacio is a sneaky pirate desperate to beat Max to the treasure. See if you can spot him lurking on every double page.

Horacio

Pink elephants

Fantastic Island is home to the only remaining pink elephants in the world. There is at least one hiding on every double page. Can you find them all?

How to sound Spanish

Some letters sound different in Spanish. Here are a few tips to help you say the difficult ones.

You never say h, but the letter j is said like the "h" in "half". Ll is like the "y" in "yes", ñ is like the first "n" in "onion", qu is like the "c" in "cat" and v is like the "b" in "bad".

Y is like the "y" in yes, unless on its own, when it is like the "e" in "me". Z is like the "th" in "this" in north or central Spain, but in southern Spain or South America it is like the "s" in "sat".

The Spanish r is rolled, it sounds a little like a dog growling. C and g only sound different when they come before "i" or "e". Then c is like z, (it sounds like "th" or "s", and g is like j, (it sounds like "h").

The signs ¿ and ¡ are used in written Spanish, to introduce a question or exclamation, as in ¿Qué isla? Which island? or ¡Qué raro! How strange!

El puerto The port

La aventura de Max empieza una mañana temprano.
Max's adventure starts early one morning.

Sale en su barquito rojo.
He sets off in his little red boat.

Dice adiós a sus padres, a su hermana y a su abuela.
He says goodbye to his parents, his sister and his grandma.

De repente, piensa en algo que le preocupa.
Suddenly, he thinks of something that worries him.

No sabe dónde está la Isla Fantástica.
He does not know where Fantastic Island is.

**Look at what people in the port are saying.
Can you spot what each of them can see?
Which person may be
able to help Max?**

Key 🔑

adiós	goodbye
buen viaje	have a good journey
yo veo	I see
un faro	a lighthouse
una cometa	a kite
una bicicleta	a bicycle
una isla	an island
una sirena	a mermaid
una foca	a seal
un gato	a cat
un pañuelo	a handkerchief
un ancla	an anchor
no ... nada	nothing

¿Qué isla? Which island?

Max llega en seguida a un pequeño grupo de islas.
Max soon arrives at a small group of islands.

Mira con sus prismáticos.
He looks through his binoculars.

Las islas se parecen mucho. "¿Cuál es la Isla Fantástica?"
se pregunta. De repente Morgan chilla: "¡Escucha!"
The islands all look the same. "Which one is Fantastic
Island?" he wonders. Suddenly Percival squawks: "Listen!"

"Oigo voces," dice Max, "y todas hablan de elefantes.
¡Qué raro!"
 "I can hear voices," says Max, "and they're all talking
about elephants. How strange!"

**Can you tell which island is which from what
the animals are saying?**

Key 🔑	
en	on
la isla (de)	island
la manzana	apple
la cereza	cherry
la naranja	orange
la fresa	strawberry
la frambuesa	raspberry
fantástica	fantastic
hay	there is/there are
no hay	there are no
(el/los) elefante(s)	elephant(s)
un	one/a/an
dos	two
amarillo	yellow
rojo	red
rosa	pink
gris, grises	grey
violeta	purple
y	and

En la isla de la
Manzana, hay un
elefante gris.

En la isla de la Cereza,
hay un elefante violeta y
un elefante amarillo.

En la isla de
la Naranja, no hay
elefantes.

6

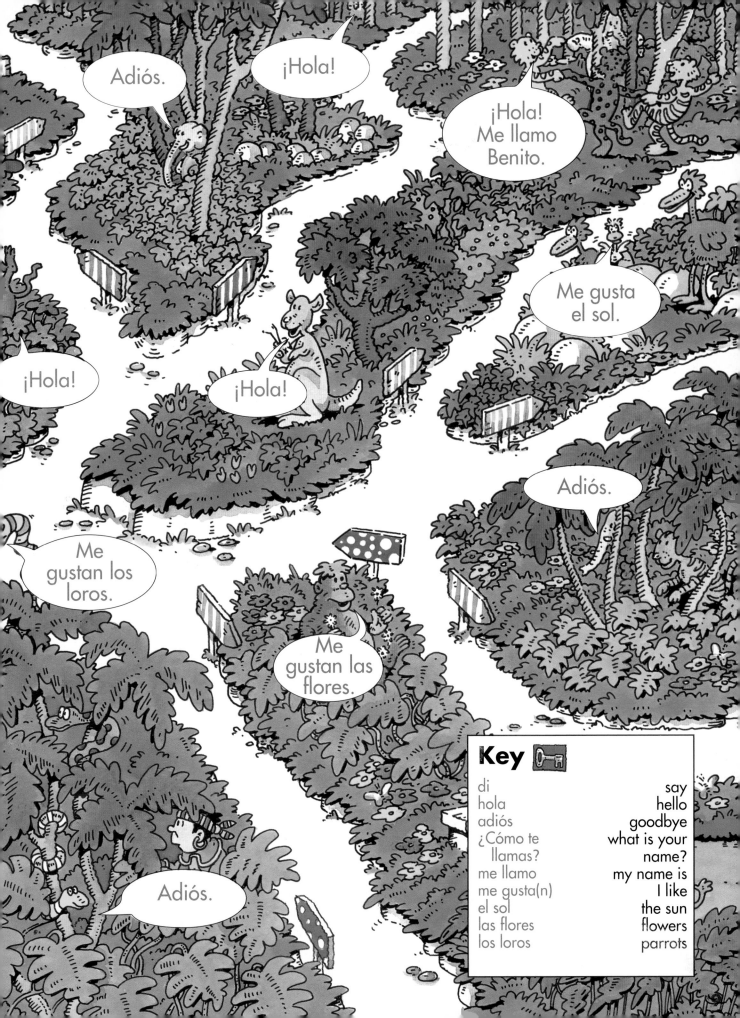

Key 🔑

di	say
hola	hello
adiós	goodbye
¿Cómo te llamas?	what is your name?
me llamo	my name is
me gusta(n)	I like
el sol	the sun
las flores	flowers
los loros	parrots

El lago   The lake

Max llega en seguida a un lago cubierto de hojas gigantes.
Max soon reaches a lake covered with giant leaves.

Decide cruzarlo saltando de hoja en hoja.
He decides to cross it by leaping from leaf to leaf.

Max descubre un cartel en medio del lago. El cartel dice que debe seguir las hojas marcadas del uno al veinte.
Max spots a sign in the middle of the lake. The sign says he must follow the leaves marked one to twenty.

Max mira alrededor desesperado. Todas las hojas parecen numeradas. ¿Cuáles debe pisar para cruzar el lago?
Max looks around in despair. All the leaves seem to be numbered. Which ones should he step on to cross the lake?

Can you help Max count to twenty on the leaves to find the right way across the lake?

Key

sigue	follow
los números	the numbers
del	from
al	to
uno	one
dos	two
tres	three
cuatro	four
cinco	five
seis	six
siete	seven
ocho	eight
nueve	nine
diez	ten
once	eleven
doce	twelve
trece	thirteen
catorce	fourteen
quince	fifteen
dieciséis	sixteen
diecisiete	seventeen
dieciocho	eighteen
diecinueve	nineteen
veinte	twenty

Sigue los números del uno al veinte.

En el bosque   In the forest

Al otro lado del lago, Max ve una cosa muy rara.
On the other side of the lake, Max sees something very odd.

Un hombre está mirando desde lo alto de una gran torre.
A man is watching from the top of a big tower.

"¡Hola!" grita Max. "¿Sabe usted dónde está el tesoro?"
"Hello!" shouts Max. "Do you know where the treasure is?"

"Sí," responde el hombre, "te lo diré, pero antes, ayúdame."
"Yes," answers the man, "I'll tell you, but first, help me."

"Estoy buscando los seis últimos animales de mi libro de
Animales Extraordinarios."
"I am looking for the last six animals in my book of
Amazing Animals."

**Can you spot all the animals the man
is looking for somewhere in the forest?**

Estoy buscando un
león, un tigre, una jirafa,
un mono, una serpiente
y un perro.

Silencio por favor.
No molestar.

Key 🔑

estoy buscando	I am looking for
no molestar	do not disturb
un león	a lion
un tigre	a tiger
una jirafa	a giraffe
un mono	a monkey
una serpiente	a snake
un perro	a dog
y	and
(el) silencio	silence
por favor	please

En el huerto In the orchard

El viejo le dice a Max en qué arbusto encontrará la siguiente pista.
The old man tells Max in which bush he will find the next clue.

Es una llave.
It is a key.

Where does the label on the key tell Max to go?

Cuando Max entra en el huerto, oye un ruido.
As Max enters the orchard, he hears a noise.

Un mono azul murmura algo.
A blue monkey is muttering something.

Should Max trust what the monkey says?

De repente, Horacio salta de detrás de un árbol.
Suddenly, Horacio leaps out from behind a tree.

Le pone a Max una red sobre la cabeza.
He puts a net over Max's head.

What is Horacio going to do?

14

Max se quita la red, pero Horacio ya ha desaparecido.
Max takes off the net, but Horacio has already disappeared.

Después oye más cuchicheos.
Then he hears more muttering.

Where does the statue tell Max to go?

Max sale hacia el Castillo Fantástico. En seguida llega a un claro.
Max sets off for Fantastic Castle. He soon comes to a clearing.

Delante de él se levantan tres castillos.
In front of him stand three castles.

Can you use the statue's directions to answer Max's question for him?

Key 🗝

voy a	I am going
vete	go
yo miento	I lie
no … nunca	never
siempre	always
¿cuál es …?	which is…?
no es	it is not
encontrar	to find
el tesoro	the treasure
al	to the
(el) huerto	orchard
(el) castillo	castle
rojo	red
amarillo	yellow
antes que	before
tú	you

15

El Castillo Fantástico   Fantastic Castle

Max llega al castillo azul.
La puerta está cerrada con llave.
Max arrives at the blue castle.
The gate is locked.

"Éste debe ser el Castillo Fantástico,"
suspira Max. "¿Pero cómo voy
a entrar?"

"This must be Fantastic Castle,"
sighs Max. "But how am I
going to get in?"

Necesito
una llave.

Tengo sed y quisiera
un chocolate.

Tengo
hambre. Quisiera
un pastel.

Max deja en el suelo su bolso que
pesa mucho. "Vamos a ver, tal vez
pueda encontrar algo útil en mi bolso."
Max puts down his heavy bag. "Let's see,
perhaps I can find something useful in my bag."

**Look at the contents of Max's bag. Can you find all the
things the weary adventurers need to keep them going?**

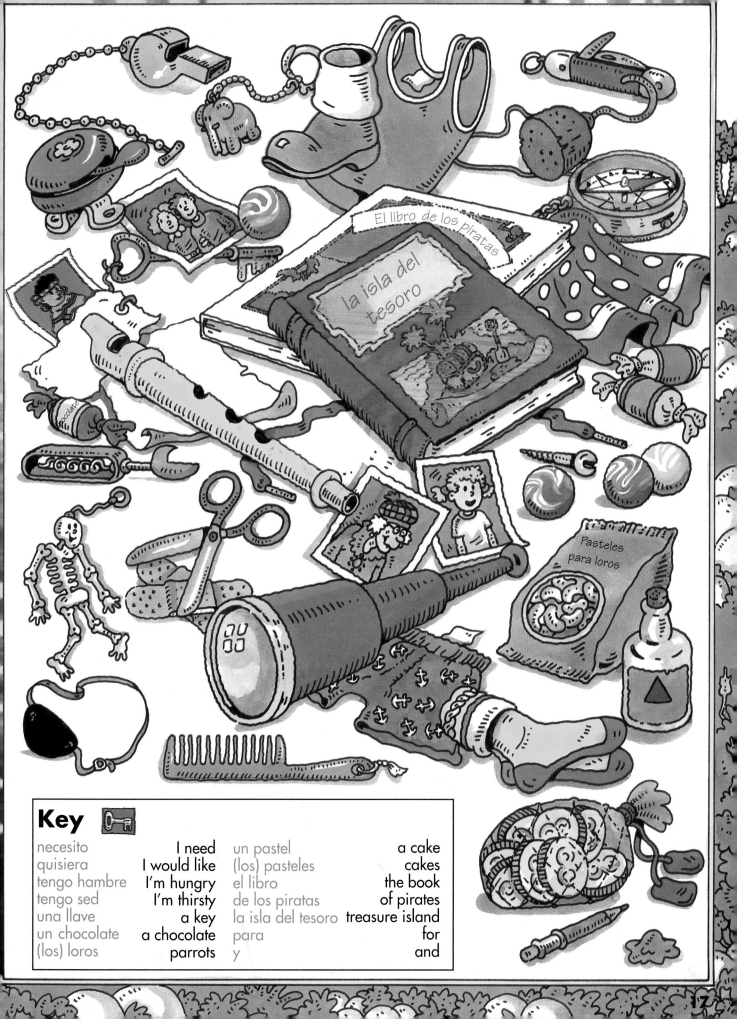

El libro de los piratas

la isla del tesoro

Pasteles para loros

17

La guarida de los piratas
The pirate's den

La llave abre fácilmente la puerta. Max y los loros buscan por el castillo.

The key opens the gate easily. Max and the parrots search the castle.

Cuando entran en la última habitación, Max exclama, "¡Es la guarida de un pirata. Casi hemos llegado!"

As they enter the last room, Max exclaims, "This is a pirate's den. We're nearly there!"

"Pero ¿cuál es la puerta para encontrar el tesoro?"

"But which is the right door for the treasure?"

Los ratones del pirata quieren ayudarle. Por desgracia para Max, son un poco cortos de vista.

The pirate's mice want to help him. Unluckily for Max, they are a little near-sighted.

The correct door is the only one which fits one of the mice's descriptions. Which door is it?

El tesoro The treasure

Max abre la puerta. Ve un camino y lo sigue hasta llegar a una enorme cascada.
Max opens the door. He sees a path and follows it to a huge waterfall.

"¡Mira!" grita a Morgan. "Una cruz en el suelo. Vamos a cavar aquí."
"Look!" he yells to Morgan. "A cross on the ground. Let's dig here."

Mientras está cavando, Max se da cuenta de que hay gente mirando.
As he digs, Max realizes that people are watching.

What are they all telling Max to do?

Key 🔑

de prisa	quick
date prisa	hurry up
estoy buscando	I am looking for
un reloj	a watch
una moto	a motorcycle
un coche	a car
una pelota	a ball
una peluca	a wig
una insignia	a badge
una calavera	a skull
(los) patines	roller skates
unos	some
con	with

De repente, la pala de Max golpea algo duro.
¡El cofre del tesoro!
Suddenly, Max's spade hits something hard.
The treasure chest!

Todo el mundo se apresura para ayudar a Max a
sacar el cofre.
Everyone hurries to help Max lift out the chest.

Max salta de alegría. Por fin es un verdadero pirata y
además tiene muchos nuevos amigos.
Max leaps for joy. At last he is a real pirate
and he has lots of new friends as well.

**Can you spot all the things that Max
and his new friends are looking for?**

Answers

Pages 4-5
The objects that people can see are circled. This lookout may be able to help Max.

Pages 6-7
Here you can see which island is which.

La isla de la Frambuesa
La isla Fantástica
La isla de la Manzana
La isla de la Naranja
La isla de la Cereza
La isla de la Fresa

Pages 8-9
The path Max should take is shown in black.

Pages 10-11
The leaves Max should step on are shown by the black line.

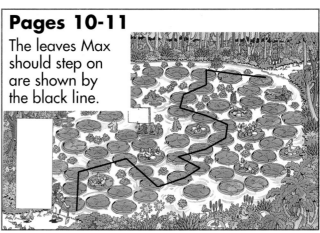

Pages 12-13
The animals the old man is looking for are circled.

Pages 14-15
The label tells Max to go to the orchard. He should not trust what the monkey says because the monkey always lies. Horacio says he is going to find the treasure before Max. The statue tells Max to go to Fantastic Castle. Fantastic Castle is the blue castle.

Pages 16-17
The things Max and the parrots need are circled.

Pages 18-19
This is the correct door.

This mouse gives the right description.

Pages 20-21
Everyone is telling Max to hurry up. The things that Max and his new friends are looking for are circled.

Did you spot everything?

Pages	Pink elephants	Equipment
4-5	two	pirate boot
6-7	one	fortifying juice
8-9	six	telescope
10-11	two	gold earring
12-13	three	hook
14-15	two	gold coins
16-17	three	parrot's brush
18-19	two	cutlass
20-21	three	pirate hat

Did you remember to find Horacio? Look back and spot him on every double page.

Word list and pronunciation guide

Here is a list of all the Spanish words and phrases used in this book. All the naming words (nouns) have el, la, los or las before them. These all mean "the". Spanish nouns are either masculine or feminine. You use el and los with masculine nouns, and la and las with feminine nouns. When you see los or las, it means the noun is plural (more than one).

Spanish describing words (adjectives) ending in o change to a when they describe feminine nouns. Here, the masculine version is written first, followed by /a, for example rojo/a (red). When an adjective describes a plural noun, it usually has an s after the o or a, for example las flores rojas (red flowers).

Each Spanish word in this list has its pronunciation shown after it *(in letters like this)*. Read these letters as if they were English words. The ones that are underlined should be said slightly louder than the rest. In South America or southern Spain, the "th" sound shown here is pronounced as "ss". For more about how to say Spanish words, see page 3.

a	*a*	to OR at
abre	*abray*	open OR (he/she) opens
la abuela	*la abwella*	grandmother
además	*ademass*	as well
adiós	*adeeyoss*	goodbye
¡ajá!	*aha*	ha! ha!
al	*al*	to the
la alegría	*la alegreeya*	joy
algo	*algo*	something
algún, alguna	*algoon, algoona*	some
alrededor	*alrededor*	around
amarillo/a	*amareelyo/a*	yellow
el amigo, la amiga	*el ameego, la ameega*	friend (boy, girl)
anaranjado/a	*anaranhado/a*	orange
el ancla	*el ankla*	anchor
los animales	*loss aneemaless*	animals
antes	*antess*	before OR first
aquí	*akee*	here
el árbol	*el arbol*	tree
el arbusto	*el arboosto*	bush
la aventura	*la abentoora*	adventure
ayúdame	*ayoodamay*	help me
ayudar	*ayoodar*	to help
azul	*athool*	blue
el barco	*el barko*	boat
el barquito	*el barkeeto*	little boat
la bicicleta	*la beetheekleta*	bike
blanco/a	*blanko/a*	white
la bolsa	*la bolsa*	bag
el bolso	*el bolso*	bag OR handbag
el bosque	*el bosskay*	forest
la bota	*la bota*	boot
la botella	*la botelya*	bottle
buen viaje	*bwen bee-a-hay*	have a good journey
buscan	*boosskan*	(they) search
buscando	*boosskando*	looking for
buscar	*boosskar*	to search OR look for
la búsqueda	*la boosskeda*	hunt OR search
la cabeza	*la kabetha*	head
la calavera	*la kalabaira*	skull (and crossbones)
el camino	*el kameeno*	path
el cartel	*el kartel*	sign
la cascada	*la kasskada*	waterfall
casi	*kassee*	almost OR nearly
el castillo	*el kassteelyo*	castle
catorce	*katorthay*	fourteen

cavando	*kabando*	digging
cavar	*kabar*	to dig
el cepillo	*el thepeelyo*	brush
la cereza	*la theretha*	cherry
cerrado/a	*therrado/a*	closed
chilla	*cheelya*	(he/she) squawks
el chocolate	*el chokolatay*	chocolate
cinco	*theenko*	five
el claro	*el klaro*	clearing
el coche	*el kochay*	car
el cofre	*el kofray*	chest
la cometa	*la kometa*	kite
comienza	*komeeyentha*	(he/she/it) begins
¿cómo?	*komo*	how?
¿cómo te llamas?	*komo tay lyamass*	what is your name?
con	*kon*	with
conducen	*kondoothen*	(they) lead
confundido/a	*konfoondeedo/a*	puzzled
convertirse en	*konbairteerssay en*	to become
el corazón	*el korathon*	heart
cortos de vista	*kortoss day beessta*	near-sighted
la cosa	*la kossa*	thing
la cruz	*la krooth*	cross
cruzar	*kroothar*	to cross
¿cuál?	*kwal*	which (one)?
¿cuáles?	*kwaless*	which (ones)?
cuando	*kwando*	when
cuatro	*kwatro*	four
cubierto/a	*koobeeyairto/a*	covered
los cuchicheos	*loss koocheechayoss*	muttering
date prisa	*datay preessa*	hurry up
de	*day*	of OR from
de prisa	*day preessa*	quickly
de pronto	*day pronto*	at once
de repente	*day repentay*	suddenly
debe	*debay*	(he/she) must
debo	*debo*	I must
decide	*detheeday*	(he/she) decides
deja	*deha*	(he/she) leaves
del	*del*	of the OR from
delante de	*daylantay day*	in front of
desaparecido	*dessaparetheedo*	disappeared
descubre	*desskoobray*	(he/she) discovers OR spots
desde lo alto	*dezday lo alto*	from the top
desesperado	*dessessperado*	in despair
después	*desspwess*	after OR then
detrás de	*detrass day*	behind

23

Spanish	Pronunciation	English
di	_dee_	say
dice	_deethay_	(he/she) says
diecinueve	dee-ethee-_nwebay_	nineteen
dieciocho	dee-ethee-_ocho_	eighteen
dieciséis	dee-ethee-_sayss_	sixteen
diecisiete	dee-ethee-see-_etay_	seventeen
diez	_dee-eth_	ten
diré	_deeray_	I will say
doce	_dothay_	twelve
¿dónde?	_donday_	where?
dos	_doss_	two
duro	_dooro_	hard
el	_el_	the
él	_el_	he OR him
el elefante	el ele_fantay_	elephant
empieza	empee-_etha_	(he/she/it) starts
en	_en_	in OR on
en seguida	en se_geeda_	soon OR right away
encontrar	enkon_trar_	to find
encontrará	enkon_trara_	(he/she) will find
enorme	e_normay_	huge
entra	_entra_	(he/she) enters
entrar	en_trar_	to enter
el equipo	el e_keepo_	equipment
es	_ess_	(he/she/it) is
escondido/a	esskon_deedo_/a	hidden
escrito/a	ess_kreeto_/a	written
escucha	ess_koocha_	listen OR (he/she) listens
eso	_esso_	that
está	_essta_	(he/she/it) is
están	_esstan_	(they) are
éste	_esstay_	this
estoy	_esstoy_	I am
exclama	ex_klama_	(he/she) exclaims
extraordinario/a(s)	extra-ordeenaree-o/a(ss)	amazing OR extraordinary
fácilmente	fatheel_mentay_	easily
fantástico/a	fantass_teeko_/a	fantastic
el faro	el _faro_	lighthouse
las flores	lass _floress_	flowers
la foca	la _foka_	seal
fortalecedor/a	fortale_thedor_/a	fortifying
la frambuesa	la fram_bwessa_	raspberry
la fresa	la _fressa_	strawberry
el garfio	el _garfee_-o	hook
el gato	el _gato_	cat
la gente	la _hentay_	people
gigante(s)	hee_gantay_(ss)	giant
golpea	gol_paya_	(he/she) hits
gran	_gran_	big
gris, grises	_greess_, _greessess_	grey
grita	_greeta_	(he/she) yells
el grupo	el _groopo_	group
la guarida	la gwa_reeda_	den
ha	_a_	(he/she/it) has ...
la habitación	la abeetathee_yon_	room
hablan	_ablan_	(they) talk
hace	_athay_	(he/she) makes OR (he/she) does
hacer	_athair_	to make OR to do
hacia	_athee_-a	toward OR for
hasta	_asta_	until OR to
hay	_eye_	there is OR there are
hemos	_emoss_	we have ...
la hermana	la _airmana_	sister
la historia	la eess_toree_-a	story
la hoja	la _oha_	leaf
hola	_ola_	hello OR hi
el hombre	el _ombray_	man
el huerto	el _wairto_	orchard
la insignia	la eensseegnee-a	badge
la isla	la _eessla_	island
la jirafa	la hee_rafa_	giraffe
el lado	el _lado_	side
el lago	el _lago_	lake
le	_lay_	to him OR to her
el león	el _layon_	lion
el libro	el _leebro_	book
la llave	la _lyabay_	key
llega	_lyega_	(he/she) arrives (at OR reaches
llegado	_lyegado_	arrived
llegar	_lyegar_	to arrive
el loro	el _loro_	parrot
el lugar	el _loogar_	place
la mañana	la _manyana_	morning
la manzana	la _manthana_	apple
marcado/a(s)	mar_kado_/a(ss)	marked
más	_mass_	more
me gusta(n)	may _goossta_(n)	I like
me llamo	may _lyamo_	my name is
medio	_medee_-o	middle
mi	_mee_	my
miento	mee-_ento_	I lie
mientras	mee-_entrass_	while OR as
mira	_meera_	look OR (he/she/it) looks
mirando	_meerando_	looking OR watching
las monedas	lass _monedass_	coins
el mono	el _mono_	monkey
la moto	la _moto_	motorcycle
mucho/a(s)	_moocho_/a(ss)	much OR many
murmura	_moormoora_	(he/she) mutters
muy	_mooy_	very
la naranja	la na_ranha_	orange
necesito	ne_thesseeto_	I need
negro/a	_negro_/a	black
no ... nada	no ... _nada_	nothing
no ... nunca	no ... _noonka_	never
no es	no _ess_	(he/she/it) is not
no hay	no _eye_	there is/are not
no molestar	no mo_lesstar_	do not disturb
no sabe	no _sabay_	(he/she) doesn't know
nueve	_nwebay_	nine
numerado/a(s)	noome_rado_/a(ss)	numbered
los números	_noomeross_	numbers
ocho	_ocho_	eight
oigo	_oygo_	I hear
once	_onthay_	eleven
oro	_oro_	gold
otro/a	_otro_/a	other
oye	_oyay_	(he/she) hears
los padres	loss _padress_	parents